## Publisher's Note

Purchase of this book entitles you to a free trial membership in the publisher's book club at www.rarebooksclub.com. (Time limited offer.) Simply enter the barcode number from the back cover onto the membership form on our home page. The book club entitles you to select from millions of books at no additional charge. You can also download a digital copy of this and related books to read on the go. Simply enter the title or subject onto the search form to find them.

Note: This is an historic book. Pages numbers, where present in the text, refer to the first edition of the book. The table of contents or index may also refer to them.

If you have any questions, could you please be so kind as to consult our Frequently Asked Questions page at www.rarebooksclub.com/faqs.cfm? You are also welcome to contact us there.

Publisher: General Books LLC™, Memphis, TN, USA, 2012. ISBN: 9781153631020.

Credits: Distributed Proofreaders.

⭄⭄ ⭄⭄ ⭄⭄ ⭄⭄ ⭄⭄ ⭄⭄ ⭄⭄ ⭄⭄

Produced by David Widger

# THE INSIDE OF THE CUP

By Winston Churchill

## TABLE OF CONTENTS OF ALL VOLUMES:

## THE INSIDE OF THE CUP

Volume 1.

### CHAPTER I

### THE WARING PROBLEMS

I

With few exceptions, the incidents recorded in these pages take place in one of the largest cities of the United States of America, and of that portion called the Middle West,—a city once conservative and provincial, and rather proud of these qualities; but now outgrown them, and linked by lightning limited trains to other teeming centers of the modern world: a city overtaken, in recent years, by the plague which has swept our country from the Atlantic to the Pacific—Prosperity. Before its advent, the Goodriches and Gores, the the Atter- ⵏⵏⵏ ⵏⵏⵏ n a sleepy quarter of shade trees and spacious yards and muddy macadam streets, now passed away forever. Existence was decorous, marriage an irrevocable step, wives were wives, and the Authorized Version of the Bible was true from cover to cover. So Dr. Gilman preached, and so they believed.

Sunday was then a day essentially different from other days—you could tell it without looking at the calendar. The sun knew it, and changed the quality of his light the very animals, dogs and cats and horses, knew it: and most of all the children knew it, by Sunday school, by Dr. Gilman's sermon, by a dizzy afternoon connected in some of their minds with ceramics and a lack of exercise; by a cold tea, and by church bells. You were not allowed to forget it for one instant. The city suddenly became full of churches, as though they had magically been let down from heaven during Saturday night. They must have been there on week days, but few persons ever thought of them.

Among the many church bells that rang on those bygone Sundays was that of St. John's, of which Dr. Gilman, of beloved memory, was rector. Dr. Gilman was a saint, and if you had had the good luck to be baptized or married or buried by him, you were probably fortunate in an earthly as well as heavenly sense. One has to be careful not to deal exclusively in superlatives, and yet it is not an exaggeration to say that St. John's was the most beautiful and churchly edifice in the city, thanks chiefly to several gentlemen of sense, and one gentleman, at least, of taste— Mr. Horace Bentley. The vicissitudes of civil war interrupted its building; but when, in 1868, it stood completed, its stone unsoiled as yet by factory smoke, its spire delicately pointing to untainted skies, its rose window glowing above the porch, citizens on Tower Street often stopped to gaze at it diagonally across the vacant lot set in order by Mr. Thurston Gore, with the intent that the view might be unobstructed.

Little did the Goodriches and Gores, the Warings and Prestons and Atterburys and other prominent people foresee the havoc that prosperity and smoke were to play with their residential plans! One by one, sooty commerce drove them out, westward, conservative though they were, from the paradise they had created; blacker and blacker grew the gothic facade of St. John's; Thurston Gore departed, but leased his corner first for a goodly sum, his ancestors being from Connecticut; leased also the vacant lot he had beautified, where stores arose and hid the spire from Tower Street. Cable cars moved serenely up the long hill where a panting third horse had been necessary, cable cars resounded in Burton Street, between the new factory and the church where Dr. Gilman still preached of peace and the delights of the New-Jerusalem. And before you could draw your breath, the cable cars had become electric. Gray hairs began to appear in the heads of the people Dr. Gilman had married in the '60's and their children were going East to College.

## II

In the first decade of the twentieth century, Asa, Waring still clung to the imposing, early Victorian mansion in Hamilton Street. It presented an uncompromising and rather scornful front to the sister mansions with which it had hitherto been on intimate terms, now fast degenerating into a shabby gentility, seeking covertly to catch the eye of boarders, but as yet refraining from open solicitation. Their lawns were growing a little ragged, their stone steps and copings revealing cracks.

Asa Waring looked with a stern distaste upon certain aspects of modern life. And though he possessed the means to follow his friends and erstwhile neighbours into the newer paradise five miles westward, he had successfully resisted for several years a formidable campaign to uproot him. His three married daughters lived in that clean and verdant district surrounding

the Park (spelled with a capital), while Evelyn and Rex spent most of their time in the West End or at the Country Clubs. Even Mrs. Waring, who resembled a Roman matron, with her wavy white hair parted in the middle and her gentle yet classic features, sighed secretly at times at the unyielding attitude of her husband, although admiring him for it. The grandchildren drew her.

On the occasion of Sunday dinner, when they surrounded her, her heart was filled to overflowing.

The autumn sunlight, reddened somewhat by the slight haze of smoke, poured in at the high windows of the dining-room, glinted on the silver, and was split into bewildering colors by the prisms of the chandelier. Many precious extra leaves were inserted under the white cloth, and Mrs. Waring's eyes were often dimmed with happiness as she glanced along the ranks on either side until they rested on the man with whom she had chosen to pass her life. Her admiration for him had gradually grown into hero-worship. His anger, sometimes roused, had a terrible moral quality that never failed to thrill her, and the Loyal Legion button on his black frock coat seemed to her an epitome of his character. He sat for the most part silent, his remarkable, penetrating eyes, lighting under his grizzled brows, smiling at her, at the children, at the grandchildren. And sometimes he would go to the corner table, where the four littlest sat, and fetch one back to perch on his knee and pull at his white, military mustache.

It was the children's day. Uproar greeted the huge white cylinder of ice-cream borne by Katie, the senior of the elderly maids; uproar greeted the cake; and finally there was a rush for the chocolates, little tablets wrapped in tinfoil and tied with red and blue ribbon. After that, the pandemonium left the dining-room, to spread itself over the spacious house from the basement to the great playroom in the attic, where the dolls and blocks and hobby-horses of the parental generation stoically awaited the new.

Sometimes a visitor was admitted to

this sacramental feat, the dearest old gentleman in the world, with a great, high bridged nose, a slight stoop, a kindling look, and snow white hair, though the top of his head was bald. He sat on Mrs. Waring's right, and was treated with the greatest deference by the elders, and with none at all by the children, who besieged him. The bigger ones knew that he had had what is called a history; that he had been rich once, with a great mansion of his own, but now he lived on Dalton Street, almost in the slums, and worked among the poor. His name was Mr. Bentley.

He was not there on the particular Sunday when this story opens, otherwise the conversation about to be recorded would not have taken place. For St. John's Church was not often mentioned in Mr. Bentley's presence.

"Well, grandmother," said Phil Goodrich, who was the favourite son-in-law, "how was the new rector today?"

"Mr. Hodder is a remarkable young man, Phil," Mrs. Waring declared, "and delivered such a good sermon. I couldn't help wishing that you and Rex and Evelyn and George had been in church."

"Phil couldn't go," explained the unmarried and sunburned Evelyn, "he had a match on of eighteen holes with me."

Mrs. Waring sighed.

"I can't think what's got into the younger people these days that they seem so indifferent to religion. Your father's a vestryman, Phil, and I believe it has always been his hope that you would succeed him. I'm afraid Rex won't succeed his father," she added, with a touch of regret and a glance of pride at her husband. "You never go to church, Rex. Phil does."

"I got enough church at boarding-school to last me a lifetime, mother," her son replied. He was slightly older than Evelyn, and just out of college. "Besides, any heathen can get on the vestry—it's a financial board, and they're due to put Phil on some day. They're always putting him on boards."

His mother looked a little distressed.

"Rex, I wish you wouldn't talk that

way about the Church—"

"I'm sorry, mother," he said, with quick penitence. "Mr. Langmaid's a vestryman, you know, and they've only got him there because he's the best corporation lawyer in the city. He isn't exactly what you'd call orthodox. He never goes."

"We are indebted to Mr. Langmaid for Mr. Hodder." This was one of Mr. Waring's rare remarks.

Eleanor Goodrich caught her husband's eye, and smiled.

"I wonder why it is," she said, "that we are so luke-warm about church in these days? I don't mean you, Lucy, or Laureston," she added to her sister, Mrs. Grey. "You're both exemplary." Lucy bowed ironically. "But most people of our ages with whom we associate. Martha Preston, for instance. We were all brought up like the children of Jonathan Edwards. Do you remember that awful round-and-round feeling on Sunday afternoons, Sally, and only the wabbly Noah's Ark elephant to play with, right in this house? instead of THAT!" There was a bump in the hall without, and shrieks of laughter. "I'll never forget the first time it occurred to me—when I was reading Darwin—that if the ark were as large as Barnum's Circus and the Natural History Museum put together, it couldn't have held a thousandth of the species on earth. It was a blow."

"I don't know what we're coming to," exclaimed Mrs. Waring gently.

"I didn't mean to be flippant, mother," said Eleanor penitently, "but I do believe the Christian religion has got to be presented in a different way, and a more vital way, to appeal to a new generation. I am merely looking facts in the face."

"What is the Christian religion?" asked Sally's husband, George Bridges, who held a chair of history in the local flourishing university. "I've been trying to find out all my life."

"You couldn't be expected to know, George," said his wife. "You were brought up an Unitarian, and went to Harvard."

"Never mind, professor," said Phil Goodrich, in a quizzical, affectionate tone. "Take the floor and tell us what it isn't."

George Bridges smiled. He was a striking contrast in type to his square-cut and vigorous brother-in-law; very thin, with slightly protruding eyes the color of the faded blue glaze of ancient pottery, and yet humorous.

"I've had my chance, at any rate. Sally made me go last Sunday and hear Mr. Hodder."

"I can't see why you didn't like him, George," Lucy cried. "I think he's splendid."

"Oh, I like him," said Mr. Bridges.

"That's just it!" exclaimed Eleanor. "I like him. I think he's sincere. And that first Sunday he came, when I saw him get up in the pulpit and wave that long arm of his, all I could think of was a modern Savonarola. He looks one. And then, when he began to preach, it was maddening. I felt all the time that he could say something helpful, if he only would. But he didn't. It was all about the sufficiency of grace,—whatever that may be. He didn't explain it. He didn't give me one notion as to how to cope a little better with the frightful complexities of the modern lives we live, or how to stop quarrelling with Phil when he stays at the office and is late for dinner. "

"Eleanor, I think you're unjust to him," said Lucy, amid the laughter of the men of the family. "Most people in St. John's think he is a remarkable preacher."

"So were many of the Greek sophists," George Bridges observed.

"Now if it were only dear old Doctor Gilman," Eleanor continued, "I could sink back into a comfortable indifference. But every Sunday this new man stirs me up, not by what he says, but by what he is. I hoped we'd get a rector with modern ideas, who would be able to tell me what to teach my children. Little Phil and Harriet come back from Sunday school with all sorts of questions, and I feel like a hypocrite. At any rate, if Mr. Hodder hasn't done anything else, he's made me want to know."

"What do you mean by a man of modern ideas, Eleanor?" inquired Mr. Bridges, with evident relish.

Eleanor put down her coffee cup, looked at him helplessly, and smiled.

"Somebody who will present Christianity to me in such a manner that it will appeal to my reason, and enable me to assimilate it into my life."

"Good for you, Nell," said her husband, approvingly. "Come now, professor, you sit up in the University' Club all Sunday morning and discuss recondite philosophy with other learned agnostics, tell us what is the matter with Mr. Hodder's theology. That is, if it will not shock grandmother too much."

"I'm afraid I've got used to being shocked, Phil," said Mrs. Waring, with her quiet smile.

"It's unfair," Mr. Bridges protested, "to ask a prejudiced pagan like me to pronounce judgment on an honest parson who is labouring according to his lights."

"Go on, George. You shan't get out of it that way."

"Well," said George, "the trouble is, from the theological point of view, that your parson is preaching what Auguste Sabatier would call a diminished and mitigated orthodoxy."

"Great heavens!" cried Phil. "What's that?"

"It's neither fish, flesh, nor fowl, nor good red herring," the professor declared. "If Mr. Hodder were cornered he couldn't maintain that he, as a priest, has full power to forgive sins, and yet he won't assert that he hasn't. The mediaeval conception of the Church, before Luther's day, was consistent, at any rate, if you once grant the premises on which it was based."

"What premises?"

"That the Almighty had given it a charter, like an insurance company, of a monopoly of salvation on this portion of the Universe, and agreed to keep his hands off. Under this conception, the sale of indulgences, masses for the soul, and temporal power are perfectly logical —inevitable. Kings and princes derive their governments from the Church. But if we once begin to doubt the validity of this charter, as the Reformers did, the whole system flies to pieces, like sticking a pin into a soap bubble.

"That is the reason why—to change the figure—the so-called Protestant world has been gradually sliding down hill ever since the Reformation. The great majority of men are not willing to turn good, to renounce the material and sensual rewards under their hands without some definite and concrete guaranty that, if they do so, they are going, to be rewarded hereafter. They demand some sort of infallibility. And when we let go of the infallibility of the Church, we began to slide toward what looked like a bottomless pit, and we clutched at the infallibility of the Bible. And now that has begun to roll.

"What I mean by a mitigated orthodoxy is this: I am far from accusing Mr. Hodder of insincerity, but he preaches as if every word of the Bible were literally true, and had been dictated by God to the men who held the pen, as if he, as a priest, held some supernatural power that could definitely be traced, through what is known as the Apostolic Succession, back to Peter."

"Do you mean to say, George," asked Mrs. Waring, with a note of pain in her voice, "that the Apostolic Succession cannot be historically proved?"

"My dear mother," said George, "I hope you will hold me innocent of beginning this discussion. As a harmless professor of history in our renowned University (of which we think so much that we do not send our sons to it) I have been compelled by the children whom you have brought up to sit in judgment on the theology of your rector."

"They will leave us nothing!" she sighed.

"Nothing, perhaps, that was invented by man to appeal to man's superstition and weakness. Of the remainder—who can say?"

"What," asked Mrs. Waring, "do they say about the Apostolic Succession?"

"Mother is as bad as the rest of us," said Eleanor.

"Isn't she, grandfather?"

"If I had a house to rent," said Mr. Bridges, when the laughter had subsided, "I shouldn't advertise five bath rooms when there were only two, or electricity when there was only gas. I should be afraid my tenants might find it out, and lose a certain amount of confidence in me. But the orthodox churches are running just such a risk to-day, and if any person who contemplates entering these churches doesn't examine the premises first, he refrains at his own cost.

"The situation in the early Christian Church is now a matter of history, and he who runs may read. The first churches, like those of Corinth and Ephesus and Rome, were democracies: no such thing as a priestly line to carry on a hierarchy, an ecclesiastical dynasty, was dreamed of. It may be gathered from the gospels that such an idea was so far from the mind of Christ that his mission was to set at naught just such another hierarchy, which then existed in Israel. The Apostles were no more bishops than was John the Baptist, but preachers who travelled from place to place, like Paul. The congregations, at Rome and elsewhere, elected their own 'presbyteri, episcopoi' or overseers. It is, to say the least, doubtful, and it certainly cannot be proved historically, that Peter ever was in Rome."

"The professor ought to have a pulpit of his own," said Phil.

There was a silence. And then Evelyn, who had been eating quantities of hothouse grapes, spoke up.

"So far as I can see, the dilemma in which our generation finds itself is this,—we want to know what there is in Christianity that we can lay hold of. We should like to believe, but, as George says, all our education contradicts the doctrines that are most insisted upon. We don't know where to turn. We have the choice of going to people like George, who know a great deal and don't believe anything, or to clergymen like Mr. Hodder, who demand that we shall violate the reason in us which has been so carefully trained."

"Upon my word, I think you've put it rather well, Evelyn," said Eleanor, admiringly.

"In spite of personalities," added Mr. Bridges.

"I don't see the use of fussing about it," proclaimed Laureston Grey, who was the richest and sprucest of the three sons-in-law. "Why can't we let well enough alone?"

"Because it isn't well enough," Evelyn replied. "I want the real thing or nothing. I go to church once a month, to please mother. It doesn't do me any good. And I don't see what good it does you and Lucy to go every Sunday. You never think of it when you're out at dinners and dances during the week. And besides," she added, with the arrogance of modern youth, "you and Lucy are both intellectually lazy."

"I like that from you, Evelyn," her sister flared up.

"You never read anything except the sporting columns and the annual rules of tennis and golf and polo."

"Must everything be reduced to terms?" Mrs. Waring gently lamented. "Why can't we, as Laury suggests, just continue to trust?"

"They are the more fortunate, perhaps, who can, mother," George Bridges answered, with more of feeling in his voice than he was wont to show. "Unhappily, truth does not come that way. If Roger Bacon and Galileo and Newton and Darwin and Harvey and the others had 'just trusted,' the world's knowledge would still remain as stationary as it was during the thousand-odd years the hierarchy of the Church was supreme, when theology was history, philosophy, and science rolled into one. If God had not meant man to know something of his origin differing from the account in Genesis, he would not have given us Darwin and his successors. Practically every great discovery since the Revival we owe to men who, by their very desire for truth, were forced into opposition to the tremendous power of the Church, which always insisted that people should 'just trust,' and take the mixture of cosmogony and Greek philosophy, tradition and fable, paganism, Judaic sacerdotalism, and temporal power wrongly called spiritual dealt out by this same Church as the last word on science, philosophy, history, metaphysics, and government."

"Stop!" cried Eleanor. "You make me dizzy."

"Nearly all the pioneers to whom we owe our age of comparative enlightenment were heretics," George persisted. "And if they could have been headed off, or burned, most of us would still be living in mud caves at the foot of the cliff on which stood the nobleman's castle; and kings would still be kings by divine decree, scientists—if there were any —workers in the black art, and every phenomenon we failed to understand, a miracle."

"I choose the United States of America," ejaculated Evelyn.

"I gather, George," said Phil Goodrich, "that you don't believe in miracles."

"Miracles are becoming suspiciously fewer and fewer. Once, an eclipse of the sun was enough to throw men on their knees because they thought it supernatural. If they were logical they'd kneel today because it has been found natural. Only the inexplicable phenomena are miracles; and after a while—if the theologians will only permit us to finish the job —there won't be any inexplicable phenomena. Mystery, as I believe William James puts it may be called the more-to-be-known."

"In taking that attitude, George, aren't you limiting the power of God?" said Mrs. Waring.

"How does it limit the power of God, mother," her son-in-law asked, "to discover that he chooses to work by laws? The most suicidal tendency in religious bodies today is their mediaeval insistence on what they are pleased to call the supernatural. Which is the more marvellous—that God can stop the earth and make the sun appear to stand still, or that he can construct a universe of untold millions of suns with planets and satellites, each moving in its orbit, according to law; a universe wherein every atom is true to a sovereign conception? And yet this marvel of marvels—that makes God in the twentieth century infinitely greater than in the sixteenth—would never have been discovered if the champions of theology had

had their way."

Mrs. Waring smiled a little.

"You are too strong for me, George," she said, "but you mustn't expect an old woman to change."

"Mother, dear," cried Eleanor, rising and laying her hand on Mrs. Waring's cheek, "we don't want you to change. It's ourselves we wish to change, we wish for a religious faith like yours, only the same teaching which gave it to you is powerless for us. That's our trouble. We have only to look at you," she added, a little wistfully, "to be sure there is something—something vital in Christianity, if we could only get at it, something that does not depend upon what we have been led to believe is indispensable. George, and men like him, can only show the weakness in the old supports. I don't mean that they aren't doing the world a service in revealing errors, but they cannot reconstruct."

"That is the clergyman's business," declared Mr. Bridges. "But he must first acknowledge that the old supports are worthless."

"Well," said Phil, "I like your rector, in spite of his anthropomorphism —perhaps, as George would say, because of it. There is something manly about him that appeals to me."

"There," cried Eleanor, triumphantly, "I've always said Mr. Hodder had a spiritual personality. You feel—you feel there is truth shut up inside of him which he cannot communicate. I'll tell you who impresses me in that way more strongly than any one else—Mr. Bentley. And he doesn't come to church any more."

"Mr. Bentley," said her, mother, "is a saint. Your father tried to get him to dinner to-day, but he had promised those working girls of his, who live on the upper floors of his house, to dine with them. One of them told me so. Of course he will never speak of his kindnesses."

"Mr. Bentley doesn't bother his head about theology," said Sally. "He just lives."

"There's Eldon Parr," suggested George Bridges, mentioning the name of the city's famous financier; "I'm told

he relieved Mr. Bentley of his property some twenty-five years ago. If Mr. Hodder should begin to preach the modern heresy which you desire, Mr Parr might object. He's very orthodox, I'm told."

"And Mr. Parr," remarked the modern Evelyn, sententiously, "pays the bills, at St. John's. Doesn't he, father?"

"I fear he pays a large proportion of them," Mr. Waring admitted, in a serious tone.

"In these days," said Evelyn, "the man who pays the bills is entitled to have his religion as he likes it."

"No matter how he got the money to pay them," added Phil.

"That suggests another little hitch in the modern church which will have to be straightened out," said George Bridges.

"'Woe unto you, scribes and Pharisees, hypocrites! For ye make clean the outside of the cup and of the platter, but within they are full of extortion and excess.'"

"Why, George, you of all people quoting the Bible!" Eleanor exclaimed.

"And quoting it aptly, too," said Phil Goodrich.

"I'm afraid if we began on the scribes and Pharisees, we shouldn't stop with Mr. Parr," Asa Wiring observed, with a touch of sadness.

"In spite of all they say he has done, I can't help feeling sorry for him," said Mrs. Waring. "He must be so lonely in that huge palace of his beside the Park, his wife dead, and Preston running wild around the world, and Alison no comfort. The idea of a girl leaving her father as she did and going off to New York to become a landscape architect!"

"But, mother," Evelyn pleaded, "I can't see why a woman shouldn't lead her own life. She only has one, like a man. And generally she doesn't get that."

Mrs. Waring rose.

"I don't know what we're coming to. I was taught that a woman's place was with her husband and children; or, if she had none, with her family. I tried to teach you so, my dear."

"Well," said Evelyn, "I'm here yet. I haven't Alison's excuse. Cheer up, mother, the world's no worse than it was."

"I don't know about that," answered Mrs. Waring.

"Listen!" ejaculated Eleanor.

Mrs. Waring's face brightened. Sounds of mad revelry came down from the floor above.

## CHAPTER II

### MR. LANGMAID'S MISSION

**I**

Looking back over an extraordinary career, it is interesting to attempt to fix the time when a name becomes a talisman, and passes current for power. This is peculiarly difficult in the case of Eldon Parr. Like many notable men before him, nobody but Mr. Parr himself suspected his future greatness, and he kept the secret. But if we are to search what is now ancient history for a turning-point, perhaps we should find it in the sudden acquisition by him of the property of Mr. Bentley.

The transaction was a simple one. Those were the days when gentlemen, as matters of courtesy, put their names on other gentlemen's notes; and modern financiers, while they might be sorry for Mr. Bentley, would probably be unanimous in the opinion that he was foolish to write on the back of Thomas Garrett's. Mr. Parr was then, as now, a business man, and could scarcely be expected to introduce philanthropy into finance. Such had been Mr. Bentley's unfortunate practice. And it had so happened, a few years before, for the accommodation of some young men of his acquaintance that he had invested rather generously in Grantham mining stock at twenty-five cents a share, and had promptly forgotten the transaction. To cut a long story short, in addition to Mr. Bentley's house and other effects, Mr. Parr became the owner of the Grantham stock, which not long after went to one hundred dollars. The reader may do the figuring.

Where was some talk at this time, but many things had happened since. For example, Mr. Parr had given away great sums in charity. And it may likewise be added in his favour that Mr. Bentley was glad to be rid of his fortune. He had said so. He deeded his pew back to St. John's, and protesting to his friends that he was not unhappy, he disappeared from the sight of all save a few. The rising waters of Prosperity closed over him. But Eliza Preston, now Mrs. Parr, was one of those who were never to behold him again,—in this world, at least.

She was another conspicuous triumph in that career we are depicting. Gradual indeed had been the ascent from the sweeping out of a store to the marrying of a Preston, but none the less sure inevitable. For many years after this event, Eldon Parr lived modestly in what was known as a "stone-front" house in Ransome Street, set well above the sidewalk, with a long flight of yellow stone steps leading to it; steps scrubbed with Sapoho twice a week by a negro in rubber boots. There was a stable with a tarred roof in the rear, to be discerned beyond the conventional side lawn that was broken into by the bay window of the dining-room. There, in that house, his two children were born: there, within those inartistic walls, Eliza Preston lived a life that will remain a closed book forever. What she thought, what she dreamed, if anything, will never be revealed. She did not, at least, have neurasthenia, and for all the world knew, she may have loved her exemplary and successful husband, with whom her life was as regular as the Strasburg clock. She breakfasted at eight and dined at seven; she heard her children's lessons and read them Bible stories; and at half past ten every Sunday morning, rain or shine, walked with them and her husband to the cars on Tower Street to attend service at St. John's, for Mr. Parr had scruples in those days about using the carriage on the Sabbath.

She did not live, alas, to enjoy for long the Medicean magnificence of the mansion facing the Park, to be a companion moon in the greater orbit. Eldon Part's grief was real, and the beautiful English window in the south transept of the church bears witness to it. And yet it cannot be said that he sought solace in religion, so apparently steeped in it had he always been. It was destiny that he should take his place on the vestry; destiny, indeed, that he should ultimately become the vestry as well as the first layman of the diocese; unobtrusively, as he had accomplished everything else in life, in spite of Prestons and Warings, Atterburys, Goodriches, and Gores. And he was wont to leave his weighty business affairs to shift for themselves while he attended the diocesan and general conventions of his Church.

He gave judiciously, as becomes one who holds a fortune in trust, yet generously, always permitting others to help, until St. John's was a very gem of finished beauty. And, as the Rothschilds and the Fuggera made money for grateful kings and popes, so in a democratic age, Eldon Parr became the benefactor of an adulatory public. The university, the library, the hospitals, and the parks of his chosen city bear witness.

**II**

For forty years, Dr. Gilman had been the rector of St. John's. One Sunday morning, he preached his not unfamiliar sermon on the text, "For now we see through a glass, darkly; but then face to face," and when the next Sunday dawned he was in his grave in Winterbourne Cemetery, sincerely mourned within the parish and without. In the nature of mortal things, his death was to be expected: no less real was the crisis to be faced At the vestry meeting that followed, the problem was tersely set forth by Eldon Parr, his frock coat tightly buttoned about his chest, his glasses in his hand.

"Gentlemen," he said, "we have to fulfil a grave responsibility to the parish, to the city, and to God. The matter of choosing a rector to-day, when clergymen are meddling with all sorts of affairs which do not concern them, is not so simple as it was twenty years ago. We have, at St. John's, always been orthodox and dignified, and I take it to be the sense of this vestry that we remain so. I conceive it our duty to find a man who is neither too old nor too young, who will preach the faith as we received it, who is not sensational, and who does not mistake socialism for Christianity."

By force of habit, undoubtedly, Mr. Parr glanced at Nelson Langmaid as he sat down. Innumerable had been the meetings of financial boards at which Mr. Parr had glanced at Langmaid, who had never failed to respond. He was that sine qua non of modern affairs, a corporation lawyer,—although he resembled a big and genial professor of Scandinavian extraction. He wore round, tortoise-shell spectacles, he had a high, dome-like forehead, and an ample light brown beard which he stroked from time to time. It is probable that he did not believe in the immortality of the soul.

His eyes twinkled as he rose.

"I don't pretend to be versed in theology, gentlemen, as you know," he said, and the entire vestry, even Mr. Parr, smiled. For vestries, in spite of black coats and the gravity of demeanour which first citizens are apt to possess, are human after all. "Mr. Parr has stated, I believe; the requirements, and I agree with him that it is not an easy order to fill. You want a parson who will stick to his last, who will not try experiments, who is not too high or too low or too broad or too narrow, who has intellect without too much initiative, who can deliver a good sermon to those who can appreciate one, and yet will not get the church uncomfortably full of strangers and run you out of your pews. In short, you want a level-headed clergyman about thirty-five years old who will mind his own business"

The smiles on the faces of the vestry deepened. The ability to put a matter thus humorously was a part of Nelson Langmaid's power with men and juries.

"I venture to add another qualification," he continued, "and that is virility. We don't want a bandbox rector. Well, I happen to have in mind a young man who errs somewhat on the other side, and who looks a little like a cliff profile I once saw on Lake George of George Washington or an Indian chief, who stands about six feet two. He's a bachelor—if that's a drawback. But I am not at all sure he can be induced to leave his present parish, where he has been for

ten years."

"I am," announced Wallis Plimpton, with his hands in his pockets, "provided the right man tackles him."

### III

Nelson Langmaid's most notable achievement, before he accomplished the greater one of getting a new rector for St. John's, had been to construct the "water-tight box" whereby the Consolidated Tractions Company had become a law-proof possibility. But his was an esoteric reputation, —the greater fame had been Eldon Parr's. Men's minds had been dazzled by the breadth of the conception of scooping all the street-car lines of the city, long and short, into one big basket, as it were; and when the stock had been listed in New York, butcher and baker, clerk and proprietor, widow and maid, brought out their hoardings; the great project was discussed in clubs, cafes, and department stores, and by citizens hanging on the straps of the very cars that were to be consolidated—golden word! Very little appeared about Nelson Langmaid, who was philosophically content. But to Mr. Parr, who was known to dislike publicity, were devoted pages in the Sunday newspapers, with photographs of the imposing front of his house in Park Street, his altar and window in St. John's, the Parr building, and even of his private car, Antonia.

Later on, another kind of publicity, had come. The wind had whistled for a time, but it turned out to be only a squall. The Consolidated Tractions Company had made the voyage for which she had been constructed, and thus had fulfilled her usefulness; and the cleverest of the rats who had mistaken her for a permanent home scurried ashore before she was broken up.

All of which is merely in the nature of a commentary on Mr. Langmaid's genius. His reputation for judgment—which by some is deemed the highest of human qualities—was impaired; and a man who in his time had selected presidents of banks and trust companies could certainly be trusted to choose a parson—particularly if the chief requirements were not of a spiritual na-

ture. . .

A week later he boarded an eastbound limited train, armed with plenary powers.

His destination was the hill town where he had spent the first fifteen years of his life, amid the most striking of New England landscapes, and the sight of the steep yet delicately pastoral slopes never failed to thrill him as the train toiled up the wide valley to Bremerton. The vision of these had remained with him during the years of his toil in the growing Western city, and embodied from the first homesick days an ideal to which he hoped sometime permanently to return. But he never had. His family had shown a perversity of taste in preferring the sea, and he had perforce been content with a visit of a month or so every other summer, accompanied usually by his daughter, Helen. On such occasions, he stayed with his sister, Mrs. Whitely.

The Whitely mills were significant of the new Bremerton, now neither village nor city, but partaking of the characteristics of both. French Canadian might be heard on the main square as well as Yankee; and that revolutionary vehicle, the automobile, had inspired there a great brick edifice with a banner called the Bremerton House. Enterprising Italians had monopolized the corners with fruit stores, and plate glass and asphalt were in evidence. But the hills looked down unchanged, and in the cool, maple-shaded streets, though dotted with modern residences, were the same demure colonial houses he had known in boyhood.

He was met at the station by his sister, a large, matronly woman who invariably set the world whizzing backward for Langmaid; so completely did she typify the contentment, the point of view of an age gone by. For life presented no more complicated problems to the middle-aged Mrs. Whitely than it had to Alice Langmaid.

"I know what you've come for, Nelson," she said reproachfully, when she greeted him at the station. "Dr. Gilman's dead, and you want our Mr. Hodder. I feel it in my bones. Well, you can't get him. He's had ever so many calls, but he won't leave Bremerton."

She knew perfectly well, however, that Nelson would get him, although her brother characteristically did not at once acknowledge his mission. Alice Whitely had vivid memories of a childhood when he had never failed to get what he wanted; a trait of his of which, although it had before now caused her much discomfort, she was secretly inordinately proud. She was, therefore, later in the day not greatly surprised to find herself supplying her brother with arguments. Much as they admired and loved Mr. Hodder, they had always realized that he could not remain buried in Bremerton. His talents demanded a wider field.

"Talents!" exclaimed Langmaid, "I didn't know he had any."

"Oh, Nelson, how can you say such a thing, when you came to get him!" exclaimed his sister."

"I recommended him because I thought he had none," Langmaid declared.

"He'll be a bishop some day—every one says so," said Mrs. Whitely, indignantly.

"That reassures me," said her brother.

"I can't see why they sent you—you hardly ever go to church," she cried. "I don't mind telling you, Nelson, that the confidence men place in you is absurd."

"You've said that before," he replied. "I agree with you. I'm not going on my judgment—but on yours and Gerald's, because I know that you wouldn't put up with anything that wasn't strictly all-wool orthodox."

"I think you're irreverent," said his sister, "and it's a shame that the canons permit such persons to sit on the vestry . . . ."

"Gerald," asked Nelson Langmaid of his brother-in-law that night, after his sister and the girls had gone to bed, "are you sure that this young man's orthodox?"

"He's been here for over ten years, ever since he left the seminary, and he's never done or said anything radical yet," replied the mill owner of Bremerton. "If you don't want him, we'd be delighted to have him stay. We're not forcing him

on you, you know. What the deuce has got into you? You've talked to him for two hours, and you've sat looking at him at the dinner table for another two. I thought you were a judge of men."

Nelson Langmaid sat silent.

"I'm only urging Hodder to go for his own good," Mr. Whitely continued. "I can take you to dozens of people to-morrow morning who worship him, — people of all sorts; the cashier in the bank, men in the mills, the hotel clerk, my private stenographer—he's built up that little church from nothing at all. And you may write the Bishop, if you wish."

"How has he built up the church?" Langmaid demanded

"How? How does any clergyman buildup a church

"I don't know," Langmaid confessed. "It strikes me as quite a tour de force in these days. Does he manage to arouse enthusiasm for orthodox Christianity?"

"Well," said Gerard Whitely, "I think the service appeals. We've made it as beautiful as possible. And then Mr. Hodder goes to see these people and sits up with them, and they tell him their troubles. He's reformed one or two rather bad cases. I suppose it's the man's personality."

Ah! Langmaid exclaimed, "now you're talking!"

"I can't see what you're driving at," confessed his brother-in-law. "You're too deep for me, Nelson."

If the truth be told, Langmaid himself did not quits see. On behalf of the vestry, he offered next day to Mr. Hodder the rectorship of St. John's and that offer was taken under consideration; but there was in the lawyer's mind no doubt of the acceptance, which, in the course of a fortnight after he had returned to the West, followed.

By no means a negligible element in Nelson Langmaid's professional success had been his possession of what may called a sixth sense, and more than once, on his missions of trust, he had listened to its admonitory promptings.

At times he thought he recognized these in his conversation with the Reverend John Hodder at Bremerton,—es-

pecially in that last interview in the pleasant little study of the rectory overlooking Bremerton Lake. But the promptings were faint, and Langmaid out of his medium. He was not choosing the head of a trust company.

He himself felt the pull of the young clergyman's personality, and instinctively strove to resist it: and was more than ever struck by Mr. Hodder's resemblance to the cliff sculpture of which he had spoken at the vestry meeting.

He was rough-hewn indeed, with gray-green eyes, and hair the color of golden sand: it would not stay brushed. It was this hair that hinted most strongly of individualism, that was by no means orthodox. Langmaid felt an incongruity, but he was fascinated; and he had discovered on the rector's shelves evidences of the taste for classical authors that he himself possessed. Thus fate played with him, and the two men ranged from Euripides to Horace, from Horace to Dante and Gibbon. And when Hodder got up to fetch this or that edition, he seemed to tower over the lawyer, who was a big man himself.

Then they discussed business, Langmaid describing the parish, the people, the peculiar situation in St. John's caused by Dr. Gilman's death, while Hodder listened. He was not talkative; he made no promises; his reserve on occasions was even a little disconcerting; and it appealed to the lawyer from Hodder as a man, but somehow not as a clergyman. Nor did the rector volunteer any evidences of the soundness of his theological or political principles.

He gave Langmaid the impression—though without apparent egotism—that by accepting the call he would be conferring a favour on St. John's; and this was when he spoke with real feeling of the ties that bound him to Bremerton. Langmaid felt a certain deprecation of the fact that he was not a communicant.

For the rest, if Mr. Hodder were disposed to take himself and his profession seriously, he was by no means lacking in an appreciation of Langmaid s humour . . . .

The tempering of the lawyer's elation

as he returned homeward to report to Mr. Parr and the vestry may be best expressed by his own exclamation, which he made to himself:

"I wonder what that fellow would do if he ever got started!" A parson was, after all, a parson, and he had done his best.

## IV

A high, oozing note of the brakes, and the heavy train came to a stop. Hodder looked out of the window of the sleeper to read the sign 'Marcion' against the yellow brick of the station set down in the prairie mud, and flanked by a long row of dun-colored freight cars backed up to a factory.

The factory was flimsy, somewhat resembling a vast greenhouse with its multitudinous windows, and bore the name of a firm whose offices were in the city to which he was bound.

"We 'most in now, sah," the negro porter volunteered. "You kin see the smoke yondah."

Hodder's mood found a figure in this portentous sign whereby the city's presence was betrayed to travellers from afar,—the huge pall seemed an emblem of the weight of the city's sorrows; or again, a cloud of her own making which shut her in from the sight of heaven. Absorbed in the mad contest for life, for money and pleasure and power she felt no need to lift her eyes beyond the level of her material endeavours.

He, John Hodder, was to live under that cloud, to labour under it. The mission on which he was bound, like the prophets of old, was somehow to gain the ears of this self-absorbed population, to strike the fear of the eternal into their souls, to convince them that there was Something above and beyond that smoke which they ignored to their own peril.

Yet the task, at this nearer view, took on proportions overwhelming—so dense was that curtain at which he gazed. And to-day the very skies above it were leaden, as though Nature herself had turned atheist. In spite of the vigour with which he was endowed, in spite of the belief in his own soul, doubts assailed him of his ability to cope with this problem of the modern Nineveh— at the very moment when he was about to realize his matured ambition of a great city parish.

Leaning back on the cushioned seat, as the train started again, he reviewed the years at Bremerton, his first and only parish. Hitherto (to his surprise, since he had been prepared for trials) he had found the religious life a primrose path. Clouds had indeed rested on Bremerton's crests, but beneficent clouds, always scattered by the sun. And there, amid the dazzling snows, he had on occasions walked with God.

His success, modest though it were, had been too simple. He had loved the people, and they him, and the pang of homesickness he now experienced was the intensest sorrow he had known since he had been among them. Yes, Bremerton had been for him (he realized now that he had left it) as near an approach to Arcadia as this life permits, and the very mountains by which it was encircled had seemed effectively to shut out those monster problems which had set the modern world outside to seething. Gerald Whitely's thousand operatives had never struck; the New York newspapers, the magazines that discussed with vivid animus the corporation-political problems in other states, had found Bremerton interested, but unmoved; and Mrs. Whitely, who was a trustee of the library, wasted her energy in deploring the recent volumes on economics, sociology, philosophy, and religion that were placed on the shelves. If Bremerton read them—and a portion of Bremerton did—no difference was apparent in the attendance at Hodder's church. The Woman's Club discussed them strenuously, but made no attempt to put their doctrines into practice.

Hodder himself had but glanced at a few of them, and to do him justice this abstention had not had its root in cowardice. His life was full —his religion "worked." And the conditions with which these books dealt simply did not exist for him. The fact that there were other churches in the town less successful than his own (one or two, indeed, virtually starving) he had found it simple to account for in that their denominations had abandoned the true conception of the Church, and were logically degenerating into atrophy. What better proof of the barrenness of these modern philosophical and religious books did he need than the spectacle of other ministers—who tarried awhile on starvation salaries —reading them and preaching from them?

He, John Hodder, had held fast to the essential efficacy of the word of God as propounded in past ages by the Fathers. It is only fair to add that he did so without pride or bigotry, and with a sense of thankfulness at the simplicity of the solution (ancient, in truth!) which, apparently by special grace, had been vouchsafed him. And to it he attributed the flourishing condition in which he had left the Church of the Ascension at Bremerton.

"We'll never get another rector like you," Alice Whitely had exclaimed, with tears in her eyes, as she bade him good-by. And he had rebuked her. Others had spoken in a similar strain, and it is a certain tribute to his character to record that the underlying hint had been lost on Hodder. His efficacy, he insisted, lay in the Word.

Hodder looked at his watch, only to be reminded poignantly of the chief cause of his heaviness of spirit, for it represented concretely the affections of those whom he had left behind; brought before him vividly the purple haze of the Bremerton valley, and the garden party, in the ample Whitely grounds, which was their tribute to him. And he beheld, moving from the sunlight to shadow, the figure of Rachel Ogden. She might have been with him now, speeding by his side into the larger life!

In his loneliness, he seemed to be gazing into reproachful eyes. Nothing had passed between them. It, was he who had held back, a fact that in the retrospect caused him some amazement. For, if wifehood were to be regarded as a profession, Rachel Ogden had every qualification. And Mrs. Whitely's skilful suggestions had on occasions almost brought him to believe in the reality of the mirage,—never quite.

Orthodox though he were, there had been times when his humour had borne him upward toward higher truths, and he had once remarked that promising to love forever was like promising to become President of the United States.

One might achieve it, but it was independent of the will. Hodder's ideals—if he had only known—transcended the rubric. His feeling for Rachel Ogden had not been lacking in tenderness, and yet he had recoiled from marriage merely for the sake of getting a wife, albeit one with easy qualification. He shrank instinctively from the humdrum, and sought the heights, stormy though these might prove. As yet he had not analyzed this craving.

This he did know—for he had long ago torn from his demon the draperies of disguise—that women were his great temptation. Ordination had not destroyed it, and even during those peaceful years at Bremerton he had been forced to maintain a watchful guard. He had a power over women, and they over him, that threatened to lead him constantly into wayside paths, and often he wondered what those who listened to him from the pulpit would think if they guessed that at times, he struggled with suggestion even now. Yet, with his hatred of compromises, he had scorned marriage.

The yoke of Augustine! The caldron of unholy loves! Even now, as he sat in the train, his mind took its own flight backward into that remoter past that was still a part of him: to secret acts of his college days the thought of which made him shudder; yes, and to riots and revels. In youth, his had been one of those boiling, contagious spirits that carry with them, irresistibly, tamer companions. He had been a leader in intermittent raids into forbidden spheres; a leader also in certain more decorous pursuits—if athletics may be so accounted; yet he had capable of long periods of self-control, for a cause. Through it all a spark had miraculously been kept alive. . . .

Popularity followed him from the small New England college to the Harvard Law School. He had been soberer there, marked as a pleader, and at last the day arrived when he was summoned by a great New York lawyer to discuss his future. Sunday intervened. Obeying a wayward impulse, he had gone to one of the metropolitan churches to hear a preacher renowned for his influence over men. There is, indeed, much that is stirring to the imagination in the spectacle of a mass of human beings thronging into a great church, pouring up the aisles, crowding the galleries, joining with full voices in the hymns. What drew them? He himself was singing words familiar since childhood, and suddenly they were fraught with a startling meaning!

"Fill me, radiancy divine,
Scatter all my unbelief!"

Visions of the Crusades rose before him, of a friar arousing France, of a Maid of Orleans; of masses of soiled, war-worn, sin-worn humanity groping towards the light. Even after all these ages, the belief, the hope would not down.

Outside, a dismal February rain was falling, a rain to wet the soul. The reek of damp clothes pervaded the gallery where he sat surrounded by clerks and shop girls, and he pictured to himself the dreary rooms from which they had emerged, drawn by the mysterious fire on that altar. Was it a will-o'-the-wisp? Below him, in the pews, were the rich. Did they, too, need warmth?

Then came the sermon, "I will arise and go to my father."

After the service, far into the afternoon, he had walked the wet streets heedless of his direction, in an exaltation that he had felt before, but never with such intensity. It seemed as though he had always wished to preach, and marvelled that the perception had not come to him sooner. If the man to whom he had listened could pour the light into the dark corners of other men's souls, he, John Hodder, felt the same hot spark within him,—despite the dark corners of his own!

At dusk he came to himself, hungry, tired, and wet, in what proved to be the outskirts of Harlem. He could see the place now: the lonely, wooden houses, the ramshackle saloon, the ugly, yellow gleam from the street lamps in a line along the glistening pavement; beside him, a towering hill of granite with a real estate sign, "This lot for sale." And he had stood staring at it, thinking of the rock that would have to be cut away before a man could build there,—and so read his own parable.

How much rock would have to be cut away, how much patient chipping before the edifice of which he had been dreaming could be reared! Could he ever do it? Once removed, he would be building on rock. But could he remove it? . . . To help revive a faith, a dying faith, in a material age, —that indeed were a mission for any man! He found his way to an elevated train, and as it swept along stared unseeing at the people who pushed and jostled him. Still under the spell, he reached his room and wrote to the lawyer thanking him, but saying that he had reconsidered coming to New York. It was not until he had posted the letter, and was on his way back to Cambridge that he fully realized he had made the decision of his life.

Misgivings, many of them, had come in the months that followed, misgivings and struggles, mocking queries. Would it last? There was the incredulity and amazement of nearest friends, who tried to dissuade him from so extraordinary a proceeding. Nobody, they said, ever became a parson in these days; nobody, at least, with his ability. He was throwing himself away. Ethics had taken the place of religion; intelligent men didn't go to church. And within him went on an endless debate. Public opinion made some allowance for frailties in other professions; in the ministry, none: he would be committing himself to be good the rest of his life, and that seemed too vast an undertaking for any human.

The chief horror that haunted him was not failure,—for oddly enough he never seriously distrusted his power, it was disaster. Would God give him the strength to fight his demon? If he were to gain the heights, only to stumble in the sight of all men, to stumble and fall.

Seeming echoes of the hideous

mockery of it rang in his ears: where is the God that this man proclaimed? he saw the newspaper headlines, listened in imagination to cynical comments, beheld his name trailed through the soiled places of the cities, the shuttlecock of men and women. "To him that overcometh, to him will I give of the hidden manna, and I will give him a white stone, and upon the stone a new name written, which no one knoweth but he that receiveth it." Might he ever win that new name, eat of the hidden manna of a hidden power, become the possessor of the morning star?

Unless there be in the background a mother, no portrait of a man is complete. She explains him, is his complement. Through good mothers are men conceived of God: and with God they sit, forever yearning, forever reaching out, helpless except for him: with him, they have put a man into the world. Thus, into the Supreme Canvas, came the Virgin.

John Hodder's mother was a widow, and to her, in the white, gabled house which had sheltered stern ancestors, he travelled in the June following his experience. Standing under the fan-light of the elm-shaded doorway, she seemed a vision of the peace wherein are mingled joy and sorrow, faith and tears! A tall, quiet woman, who had learned the lesson of mothers,—how to wait and how to pray, how to be silent with a clamouring heart.

She had lived to see him established at Bremerton, to be with him there awhile . . . .

He awoke from these memories to gaze down through the criss-cross of a trestle to the twisted, turbid waters of the river far below. Beyond was the city. The train skirted for a while the hideous, soot-stained warehouses that faced the water, plunged into a lane between humming factories and clothes-draped tenements, and at last glided into semi-darkness under the high, reverberating roof of the Union Station.

# CHAPTER III

## THE PRIMROSE PATH

### I

Nelson Langmaid's extraordinary judgment appeared once more to be vindicated.

There had been, indeed, a critical, anxious moment, emphasized by the agitation of bright feminine plumes and the shifting of masculine backs into the corners of the pews. None got so far as to define to themselves why there should be an apparent incompatibility between ruggedness and orthodoxy— but there were some who hoped and more who feared. Luther had been orthodox once, Savonarola also: in appearance neither was more canonical than the new rector.

His congregation, for the most part, were not analytical. But they felt a certain anomaly in virility proclaiming tradition. It took them several Sundays to get accustomed to it.

To those who had been used for more than a quarter of a century to seeing old Dr. Gilman's gentle face under the familiar and faded dove of the sounding-board, to the deliberation of his walk, and the hesitation of his manner, the first impression of the Reverend John Hodder was somewhat startling. They felt that there should be a leisurely element in religion. He moved across the chancel with incredible swiftness, his white surplice flowing like the draperies of a moving Victory, wasted no time with the pulpit lights, announced his text in a strong and penetrating, but by no means unpleasing voice, and began to speak with the certainty of authority.

Here, in an age when a new rector had, ceased to be an all-absorbing topic in social life, was a new and somewhat exhilarating experience. And it may be privately confessed that there were some who sat in St. John's during those first weeks of his incumbency who would indignantly have repudiated the accusation that they were not good churchmen and churchwomen, and who nevertheless had queer sensations in listening to ancient doctrines set forth with Emersonian conviction. Some were courageous enough to ask themselves, in the light of this forceful presentation, whether they really did believe them as firmly as they supposed they had.

Dear old Dr. Gilman had been milder—much milder as the years gained upon him. And latterly, when he had preached, his voice had sounded like the unavailing protest of one left far behind, who called out faintly with unheeded warnings. They had loved him: but the modern world was a busy world, and Dr. Gilman did not understand it. This man was different. Here was what the Church taught, he said, and they might slight it at their peril!

It is one thing to believe one's self orthodox, and quite another to have that orthodoxy so definitely defined as to be compelled, whether or no, to look it squarely in the face and own or disown it. Some indeed, like Gordon Atterbury, stood the test; responded to the clarion call for which they had been longing. But little Everett Constable, who also sat on the vestry, was a trifle uncomfortable in being reminded that absence from the Communion Table was perilous, although he would have been the last to deny the efficacy of the Sacrament.

The new rector was plainly not a man who might be accused of policy in pandering to the tastes of a wealthy and conservative flock. But if, in the series of sermons which lasted from his advent until well after Christmas, he had deliberately consulted their prejudices, he could not have done better. It is true that he went beyond the majority of them, but into a region which they regarded as preeminently safe,—a region the soil of which was traditional. To wit: St. Paul had left to the world a consistent theology. Historical research was ignored rather than condemned. And it might reasonably have been gathered from these discourses that the main proofs of Christ's divinity lay in his Virgin Birth, his miracles, and in the fact that his body had risen from the grave, had been seen by many, and even touched. Hence unbelief had no excuse. By divine commission there were bishops, priests, and deacons in the new hierarchy, and it was through the Apostolic Succession that he, their rector, derived his sacerdotal powers. There were, no doubt, many obscure passages in the Scripture, but men's minds were finite; a catholic acceptance was imperative, and the evils of the present day —a sufficiently sweeping statement—were wholly due to deplorable lapses from such acceptance. The Apostolic teaching must be preserved, since it transcended all modern wanderings after truth. Hell, though not definitely defined in terms of flames, was no less a state of torture (future, by implication) of which fire was but a faint symbol. And he gave them clearly to understand that an unbaptized person ran no inconsiderable risk. He did not declare unqualifiedly that the Church alone had the power to save, but such was the inference.

## II

It was entirely fitting, no doubt, when the felicitations of certain of the older parishioners on his initial sermon were over, that Mr. Hodder should be carried westward to lunch with the first layman of the diocese. But Mr. Parr, as became a person of his responsibility, had been more moderate in his comment. For he had seen, in his day, many men whose promise had been unfulfilled. Tightly buttoned, silk hatted, upright, he sat in the corner of his limousine, the tasselled speaking-tube in his hand, from time to time cautioning his chauffeur.

"Carefully!" he cried. "I've told you not to drive so fast in this part of town. I've never got used to automobiles," he remarked to Hodder, "and I formerly went to church in the street-cars, but the distances have grown so great—and I have occasionally been annoyed in them."

Hodder was not given to trite acquiescence. His homely composure belied the alertness of his faculties; he was striving to adapt himself to the sudden broadening and quickening of the stream of his life, and he felt a certain excitement—although he did not betray it—in the presence of the financier. Much as he resented the thought, it was impossible for him not to realize that the man's pleasure and displeasure were

important; for, since his arrival, he had had delicate reminders of this from many sources. Recurrently, it had caused him a vague uneasiness, hinted at a problem new to him. He was jealous of the dignity of the Church, and he seemed already to have detected in Mr. Parr's manner a subtle note of patronage. Nor could Hodder's years of provincialism permit him to forget that this man with whom he was about to enter into personal relations was a capitalist of national importance.

The neighbourhood they traversed was characteristic of our rapidly expanding American cities. There were rows of dwelling houses, once ultra-respectable, now slatternly, and lawns gone grey; some of these houses had been remodelled into third-rate shops, or thrown together to make manufacturing establishments: saloons occupied all the favourable corners. Flaming posters on vacant lots announced, pictorially, dubious attractions at the theatres. It was a wonderful Indian summer day, the sunlight soft and melting; and the smoke which continually harassed this district had lifted a little, as though in deference to the Sabbath.

Hodder read the sign on a lamp post, Dalton Street. The name clung in his memory.

"We thought, some twenty years ago, of moving the church westward," said Mr. Parr, "but finally agreed to remain where we were."

The rector had a conviction on this point, and did not hesitate to state it without waiting to be enlightened as to the banker's views.

"It would seem to me a wise decision," he said, looking out of the window, and wholly absorbed in the contemplation of the evidences of misery and vice, "with this poverty at the very doors of the church."

Something in his voice impelled Eldon Parr to shoot a glance at his profile.

"Poverty is inevitable, Mr. Hodder," he declared. "The weak always sink."

Hodder's reply, whatever it might have been, was prevented by the sudden and unceremonious flight of both occupants toward the ceiling of the limou-

sine, caused by a deep pit in the asphalt.

"What are you doing, Gratton?" Mr. Parr called sharply through the tube.

Presently, the lawns began to grow brighter, the houses more cheerful, and the shops were left behind. They crossed the third great transverse artery of the city (not so long ago, Mr. Parr remarked, a quagmire), now lined by hotels and stores with alluring displays in plate glass windows and entered a wide boulevard that stretched westward straight to the great Park. This boulevard the financier recalled as a country road of clay. It was bordered by a vivid strip, of green; a row of tall and graceful lamp posts, like sentinels, marked its course; while the dwellings, set far back on either side, were for the most part large and pretentious, betraying in their many tentative styles of architecture the reaching out of a commercial nation after beauty. Some, indeed, were simple of line and restful to the trained eye.

They came to the wide entrance of the Park, so wisely preserved as a breathing place for future generations. A slight haze had gathered over the rolling forests to the westward; but this haze was not smoke. Here, in this enchanting region, the autumn sunlight was undiluted gold, the lawns, emerald, and the red gravel around the statesman's statue glistening. The automobile quickly swung into a street that skirted the Park,—if street it might be called, for it was more like a generous private driveway,—flanked on the right by fences of ornamental ironwork and high shrubbery that concealed the fore yards of dominating private residences which might: without great exaggeration, have been called palaces.

"That's Ferguson's house," volunteered Mr. Parr, indicating a marble edifice with countless windows. "He's one of your vestrymen, you know. Ferguson's Department Store." The banker's eyes twinkled a little for the first time. "You'll probably find it convenient. Most people do. Clever business man, Ferguson."

But the rector was finding difficulty in tabulating his impressions.

They turned in between two posts of

a gateway toward a huge house of rough granite. And Hodder wondered whether, in the swift onward roll of things, the time would come when this, too, would have been deemed ephemeral. With its massive walls and heavy, red-tiled roof that sloped steeply to many points, it seemed firmly planted for ages to come. It was surrounded, yet not hemmed in, by trees of a considerable age. His host explained that these had belonged to the original farm of which all this Park Street property had made a part.

They alighted under a porte-cochere with a glass roof.

"I'm sorry," said Mr. Parr, as the doors swung open and he led the way into the house, "I'm sorry I can't give you a more cheerful welcome, but my son and daughter, for their own reasons, see fit to live elsewhere."

Hodder's quick ear detected in the tone another cadence, and he glanced at Eldon Parr with a new interest . . . .

Presently they stood, face to face, across a table reduced to its smallest proportions, in the tempered light of a vast dining-room, an apartment that seemed to symbolize the fortress-like properties of wealth. The odd thought struck the clergyman that this man had made his own Tower of London, had built with his own hands the prison in which he was to end his days. The carved oaken ceiling, lofty though it was, had the effect of pressing downward, the heavy furniture matched the heavy walls, and even the silent, quick-moving servants had a watchful air.

Mr. Parr bowed his head while Hodder asked grace. They sat down.

The constraint which had characterized their conversation continued, yet there was a subtle change in the attitude of the clergyman. The financier felt this, though it could not be said that Hodder appeared more at his ease: his previous silences had been by no means awkward. Eldon Parr liked self-contained men. But his perceptions were as keen as Nelson Langmaid's, and like Langmaid, he had gradually become conscious of a certain baffling personality in the new rector of St. John's. From

time to time he was aware of the grey-green eyes curiously fixed on him, and at a loss to account for their expression. He had no thought of reading in it an element of pity. Yet pity was nevertheless in the rector's heart, and its advent was emancipating him from the limitations of provincial inexperience.

Suddenly, the financier launched forth on a series of shrewd and searching questions about Bremerton, its church, its people, its industries, and social conditions. All of which Hodder answered to his apparent satisfaction.

Coffee was brought. Hodder pushed back his chair, crossed his knees, and sat perfectly still regarding his host, his body suggesting a repose that did not interfere with his perceptive faculties.

"You don't smoke, Mr. Hodder?"

The rector smiled and shook his head. Mr. Parr selected a diminutive, yellow cigar and held it up.

"This," he said, "has been the extent of my indulgence for twenty years. They are made for me in Cuba."

Hodder smiled again, but said nothing.

"I have had a letter from your former bishop, speaking of you in the highest terms," he observed.

"The bishop is very kind."

Mr. Parr cleared his throat.

"I am considerably older than you," he went on, "and I have the future of St. John's very much at heart, Mr. Hodder. I trust you will remember this and make allowances for it as I talk to you.

"I need not remind you that you have a grave responsibility on your shoulders for so young a man, and that St. John's is the oldest parish in the diocese."

"I think I realize it, Mr. Parr," said Hodder, gravely. "It was only the opportunity of a larger work here that induced me to leave Bremerton."

"Exactly," agreed the banker. "The parish, I believe, is in good running order—I do not think you will see the necessity for many—ahem—changes. But we sadly needed an executive head. And, if I may say so, Mr. Hodder, you strike me as a man of that type, who might have made a success in a business career."

The rector smiled again.

"I am sure you could pay me no higher compliment," he answered.

For an instant Eldon Parr, as he stared at the clergyman, tightened his lips,—lips that seemed peculiarly formed for compression. Then they relaxed into what resembled a smile. If it were one, the other returned it.

"Seriously," Mr. Parr declared, "it does me good in these days to hear, from a young man, such sound doctrine as you preach. I am not one of those who believe in making concessions to agnostics and atheists. You were entirely right, in my opinion, when you said that we who belong to the Church—and of course you meant all orthodox Christians—should stand by our faith as delivered by the saints. Of course," he added, smiling, "I should not insist upon the sublapsarian view of election which I was taught in the Presbyterian Church as a boy."

Hodder laughed, but did not interrupt.

"On the other hand," Mr. Parr continued, "I have little patience with clergymen who would make religion attractive. What does it amount to —luring people into the churches on one pretext or another, sugar-coating the pill? Salvation is a more serious matter. Let the churches stick to their own. We have at St. John's a God-fearing, conservative congregation, which does not believe in taking liberties with sound and established doctrine. And I may confess to you, Mr. Hodder, that we were naturally not a little anxious about Dr. Gilman's successor, that we should not get, in spite of every precaution, a man tinged with the new and dangerous ideas so prevalent, I regret to say, among the clergy. I need scarcely add that our anxieties have been set at rest."

"That," said Hodder, "must be taken as a compliment to the dean of the theological seminary from which I graduated."

The financier stared again. But he decided that Mr. Hodder had not meant to imply that he, Mr. Parr, was attempting to supersede the dean. The answer had been modest.

"I take it for granted that you and I and all sensible men are happily. agreed that the Church should remain where she is. Let the people come to her. She should be, if I may so express it, the sheet anchor of society, our bulwark against socialism, in spite of socialists who call themselves ministers of God. The Church has lost ground—why? Because she has given ground. The sanctity of private property is being menaced, demagogues are crying out from the house-tops and inciting people against the men who have made this country what it is, who have risked their fortunes and their careers for the present prosperity. We have no longer any right, it seems, to employ whom we will in our factories and our railroads; we are not allowed to regulate our rates, although the risks were all ours. Even the women are meddling,—they are not satisfied to stay in the homes, where they belong. You agree with me?"

"As to the women," said the rector, "I have to acknowledge that I have never had any experience with the militant type of which you speak."

"I pray God you may never have," exclaimed Mr. Parr, with more feeling than he had yet shown.

"Woman's suffrage, and what is called feminism in general, have never penetrated to Bremerton. Indeed, I must confess to have been wholly out of touch with the problems to which you refer, although of course I have been aware of their existence."

"You will meet them here," said the banker, significantly.

"Yes," the rector replied thoughtfully, "I can see that. I know that the problems here will be more complicated, more modern,—more difficult. And I thoroughly agree with you that their ultimate solution is dependent on Christianity. If I did not believe,—in spite of the evident fact which you point out of the Church's lost ground, that her future will be greater than her past, I should not be a clergyman."

The quiet but firm note of faith was, not lost on the financier, and yet was not he quite sure what was to be made of it? He had a faint and fleeting sense of disquiet, which registered and was gone.

"I hope so," he said vaguely, referring perhaps to the resuscitation of which the rector spoke. He drummed on the table. "I'll go so far as to say that I, too, think that the structure can be repaired. And I believe it is the duty of the men of influence—all men of influence—to assist. I don't say that men of influence are not factors in the Church to-day, but I do say that they are not using the intelligence in this task which they bring to bear, for instance, on their business."

"Perhaps the clergy might help," Hodder suggested, and added more seriously, "I think that many of them are honestly trying to do so."

"No doubt of it. Why is it," Mr. Parr continued reflectively, "that ministers as a whole are by no means the men they were? You will pardon my frankness. When I was a boy, the minister was looked up to as an intellectual and moral force to be reckoned with. I have heard it assigned, as one reason, that in the last thirty years other careers have opened up, careers that have proved much more attractive to young men of ability."

"Business careers?" inquired the rector.

"Precisely!"

"In other words," said Hodder, with his curious smile, "the ministry gets the men who can't succeed at anything else. "

"Well, that's putting it rather strong," answered Mr. Parr, actually reddening a little. "But come now, most young men would rather be a railroad president than a bishop,—wouldn't they?"

"Most young men would," agreed Hodder, quickly, "but they are not the young men who ought to be bishops, you'll admit that."

The financier, be it recorded to his credit, did not lack appreciation of this thrust, and, for the first time, he laughed with something resembling heartiness. This laughter, in which Hodder joined, seemed suddenly to put them on a new footing—a little surprising to both.

"Come," said the financier, rising, "I'm sure you like pictures, and Langmaid tells me you have a fancy for first editions. Would you care to go to the gallery?"

"By all means," the rector assented.

Their footsteps, as they crossed the hardwood floors, echoed in the empty house. After pausing to contemplate a Millet on the stair landing, they came at last to the huge, silent gallery, where the soft but adequate light fell upon many masterpieces, ancient and modern. And it was here, while gazing at the Corots and Bonheurs, Lawrences, Romneys, Copleys, and Halses, that Hodder's sense of their owner's isolation grew almost overpowering Once, glancing over his shoulder at Mr. Parr, he surprised in his eyes an expression almost of pain.

"These pictures must give you great pleasure," he said.

"Oh," replied the banker, in a queer voice, "I'm always glad when any one appreciates them. I never come in here alone."

Hodder did not reply. They passed along to an upstairs sitting-room, which must, Hodder thought, be directly over the dining-room. Between its windows was a case containing priceless curios.

"My wife liked this room," Mr. Parr explained, as he opened the case. When they had inspected it, the rector stood for a moment gazing out at a formal garden at the back of the house. The stalks of late flowers lay withering, but here and there the leaves were still vivid, and clusters of crimson berries gleamed in the autumn sunshine. A pergola ran down the middle, and through denuded grape-vines he caught a glimpse, at the far end, of sculptured figures and curving marble benches surrounding a pool.

"What a wonderful spot!" he exclaimed.

"My daughter Alison designed it."

"She must have great talent," said the rector.

"She's gone to New York and become a landscape architect," said his host with a perceptible dryness. "Women in these days are apt to be everything except what the Lord intended them to be."

They went downstairs, and Hodder took his leave, although he felt an odd reluctance to go. Mr. Parr rang the bell.

"I'll send you down in the motor," he said.

"I'd like the exercise of walking," said the rector. "I begin to miss it already, in the city."

"You look as if you had taken a great deal of it," Mr. Parr declared, following him to the door. "I hope you'll drop in often. Even if I'm not here, the gallery and the library are at your disposal."

Their eyes met.

"You're very good," Hodder replied, and went down the steps and through the open doorway.

Lost in reflection, he walked eastward with long and rapid strides, striving to reduce to order in his mind the impressions the visit had given him, only to find them too complex, too complicated by unlooked-for emotions. Before its occurrence, he had, in spite of an inherent common sense, felt a little uneasiness over the prospective meeting with the financier. And Nelson Langmaid had hinted, good-naturedly, that it was his, Hodder's, business, to get on good terms with Mr. Parr—otherwise the rectorship of St. John's might not prove abed of roses. Although the lawyer had spoken with delicacy, he had once more misjudged his man—the result being to put Hodder on his guard. He had been the more determined not to cater to the banker.

The outcome of it all had been that the rector left him with a sense of having crossed barriers forbidden to other men, and not understanding how he had crossed them. Whether this incipient intimacy were ominous or propitious, whether there were involved in it a germ (engendered by a radical difference of temperament) capable of developing into future conflict, he could not now decide. If Eldon Parr were Procrustes he, Hodder, had fitted the bed, and to say the least, this was extraordinary, if not a little disquieting. Now and again his thoughts reverted to the garden, and to the woman who had made it. Why had she deserted?

At length, after he had been walking for nearly an hour, he halted and looked about him. He was within a few blocks of the church, a little to one side of

Tower Street, the main east and west highway of the city, in the midst of that district in which Mr. Parr had made the remark that poverty was inevitable. Slovenly and depressing at noonday, it seemed now frankly to have flung off its mask. Dusk was gathering, and with it a smoke-stained fog that lent a sickly tinge to the lights. Women slunk by him: the saloons, apparently closed, and many houses with veiled windows betrayed secret and sinister gleams. In the midst of a block rose a tall, pretentious though cheaply constructed building with the words "Hotel Albert" in flaming electric letters above an archway. Once more his eye read Dalton Street on a lamp . . . .

Hodder resumed his walk more slowly, and in a few minutes reached his rooms in the parish house.

## CHAPTER IV

### SOME RIDDLES OF THE TWENTIETH CENTURY

I Although he found the complications of a modern city parish somewhat bewildering, the new rector entered into his duties that winter with apostolic zeal. He was aware of limitations and anomalies, but his faith was boundless, his energy the subject of good-natured comment by his vestry and parishioners, whose pressing invitations' to dinners he was often compelled to refuse. There was in John Hodder something indefinable that inflamed curiosity and left it unsatisfied.

His excuse for attending these dinners, which indeed were relaxing and enjoyable, he found in the obvious duty of getting to know the most important members of his congregation. But invariably he came away from them with an inner sense of having been baffled in this object. With a few exceptions, these modern people seemed to have no time for friendship in the real meaning of the word, no desire to carry a relationship beyond a certain point. Although he was their spiritual pastor, he knew less about most of them at the end of the winter than their butlers and their maids.

They were kind, they were delightful, they were interested in him—he occa-

sionally thought—as a somewhat anachronistic phenomenon. They petted, respected him, and deferred to him. He represented to them an element in life they recognized, and which had its proper niche. What they failed to acknowledge was his point of view—and this he was wise enough not to press at dinner tables and in drawing-rooms— that religion should have the penetrability of ether; that it should be the absorbent of life. He did not have to commit the banality of reminding them of this conviction of his at their own tables; he had sufficient humour and penetration to credit them with knowing it. Nay, he went farther in his unsuspected analysis, and perceived that these beliefs made one of his chief attractions for them. It was pleasant to have authority in a black coat at one's board; to defer, if not to bend to it. The traditions of fashion demanded a clergyman in the milieu, and the more tenaciously he clung to his prerogatives, the better they liked it.

Although they were conscious of a certain pressure, which they gently resisted, they did not divine that the radiating and rugged young man cherished serious designs upon them. He did not expect to transform the world in a day, especially the modern world. He was biding his time, awaiting individual opportunities.

They talked to him of the parish work, congratulated him on the vigour with which he had attacked it, and often declared themselves jealous of it because it claimed too much of him. Dear Dr. Gilman, they said, had had neither the strength nor the perception of 'modern needs; and McCrae, the first assistant clergyman, while a good man, was a plodder and lacking in imagination. They talked sympathetically about the problems of the poor. And some of them—particularly Mrs. Wallis Plimpton were inclined to think Hodder's replies a trifle noncommittal. The trouble, although he did not tell them so, was that he himself had by no means solved the problem. And he felt a certain reluctance to discuss the riddle of poverty over champagne and porcelain.

Mrs. Plimpton and Mrs. Constable, Mrs. Ferguson, Mrs. Langmaid, Mrs. Larrabbee, Mrs. Atterbury, Mrs. Grey, and many other ladies and their daughters were honorary members of his guilds and societies, and found time in their busy lives to decorate the church, adorn the altar, care for the vestments, and visit the parish house. Some of them did more: Mrs. Larrabbee, for instance, when she was in town, often graced the girls' classes with her presence, which was a little disquieting to the daughters of immigrants: a little disquieting, too, to John Hodder. During the three years that had elapsed since Mr. Larrabbee's death, she had, with characteristic grace and ease, taken up philanthropy; become, in particular, the feminine patron saint of Galt House, non-sectarian, a rescue home for the erring of her sex.

There were, too, in this higher realm of wealth in and out of which Hodder plunged, women like Mrs. Constable (much older than Mrs. Larrabbee) with whom philanthropy and what is known as "church work" had become second nature in a well-ordered life, and who attended with praiseworthy regularity the meetings of charitable boards and committees, not infrequently taking an interest in individuals in Mr. Hodder's classes. With her, on occasions, he did discuss such matters, only to come away from her with his bewilderment deepened.

It was only natural that he should have his moods of depression. But the recurrent flow of his energy swept them away. Cynicism had no place in his militant Christianity, and yet there were times when he wondered whether these good people really wished achievements from their rector. They had the air of saying "Bravo!" and then of turning away. And he did not conceal from himself that he was really doing nothing but labour. The distances were great; and between his dinner parties, classes, services, and visits, he was forced to sit far into the night preparing his sermons, when his brain was not so keen as it might have been. Indeed—and this thought was cynical and out of char-

acter—he asked himself on one occasion whether his principal achievement so far had not consisted in getting on unusual terms with Eldon Parr. They were not lacking who thought so, and who did not hesitate to imply it. They evidently regarded his growing intimacy with the banker with approval, as in some sort a supreme qualification for a rector of St. John's, and a proof of unusual abilities. There could be no question, for instance, that he had advanced perceptibly in the estimation of the wife of another of his vestrymen, Mrs. Wallis Plimpton.

The daughter of Thurston Gore, with all her astuteness and real estate, was of a naivete in regard to spiritual matters that Hodder had grown to recognize as impermeable. In an evening gown, with a string of large pearls testing on her firm and glowing neck, she appeared a concrete refutation of the notion of rebirth, the triumph of an unconscious philosophy of material common-sense. However, in parish house affairs, Hodder had found her practical brain of no slight assistance.

"I think it quite wonderful," she remarked, on the occasion at which he was the guest of honour in what was still called the new Gore mansion, "that you have come to know Mr. Parr so well in such a short time. How did you do it, Mr. Hodder? Of course Wallis knows him, and sees a great deal of him in business matters. He relies on Wallis. But they tell me you have grown more intimate with him than any one has been since Alison left him."

There is, in Proverbs or Ecclesiastes, a formula for answering people in accordance with their point of view. The rector modestly disclaimed intimacy. And he curbed his curiosity about Alison for the reason that he preferred to hear her story from another source.

"Oh, but you are intimate!" Mrs. Plimpton protested. "Everybody says so—that Mr. Parr sends for you all the time. What is he like when he's alone, and relaxed? Is he ever relaxed?" The lady had a habit of not waiting for answers to her questions. "Do you know, it stirs my imagination tremendously

when I think of all the power that man has. I suppose you know he has become one of a very small group of men who control this country, and naturally he has been cruelly maligned. All he has to do is to say a word to his secretary, and he can make men or ruin them. It isn't that he does ruin them—I don't mean that. He uses his wealth, Wallis says, to maintain the prosperity of the nation! He feels his trusteeship. And he is so generous! He has given a great deal to the church, and now," she added, "I am sure he will give more."

Hodder was appalled. He felt helpless before the weight of this onslaught.

"I dare say he will continue to assist, as he has in the past," he managed to say.

"Of course it's your disinterestedness," she proclaimed, examining him frankly. "He feels that you don't want anything. You always strike me as so splendidly impartial, Mr. Hodder."

Fortunately, he was spared an answer. Mr. Plimpton, who was wont to apply his gifts as a toastmaster to his own festivals, hailed him from the other end of the table.

And Nelson Langmaid, who had fallen into the habit of dropping into Hodder's rooms in the parish house on his way uptown for a chat about books, had been struck by the rector's friendship with the banker.

"I don't understand how you managed it, Hodder, in such a short time," he declared. "Mr. Parr's a difficult man. In all these years, I've been closer to him than any one else, and I don't know him today half as well as you do."

"I didn't manage it," said Hodder, briefly.

"Well," replied the lawyer, quizzically, "you needn't eat me up. I'm sure you didn't do it on purpose. If you had,—to use a Hibernian phrase,—you never would have done it. I've seen it tried before. To tell you the truth, after I'd come back from Bremerton, that was the one thing I was afraid of—that you mightn't get along with him."

Hodder himself was at a loss to account for the relationship. It troubled him vaguely, for Mr. Parr was the aggressor; and often at dusk, when Hodder was working under his study lamp, the telephone would ring, and on taking down the receiver he would hear the banker's voice. "I'm alone to-night, Mr. Hodder. Will you come and have dinner with me?"

Had he known it, this was a different method of communication than that which the financier usually employed, one which should have flattered him. If Wallis Plimpton, for instance, had received such a personal message, the fact would not have remained unknown the next day at his club. Sometimes it was impossible for Hodder to go, and he said so; but he always went when he could.

The unwonted note of appeal (which the telephone seemed somehow to enhance) in Mr. Parr's voice, never failed to find a response in the rector's heart, and he would ponder over it as he walked across to Tower Street to take the electric car for the six-mile trip westward.

This note of appeal he inevitably contrasted with the dry, matter-of-fact reserve of his greeting at the great house, which loomed all the greater in the darkness. Unsatisfactory, from many points of view, as these evenings were, they served to keep whetted Hodder's curiosity as to the life of this extraordinary man. All of its vaster significance for the world, its tremendous machinery, was out of his sight.

Mr. Parr seemed indeed to regard the rest of his fellow-creatures with the suspicion at which Langmaid had hinted, to look askance at the amenities people tentatively held out to him. And the private watchman whom Hodder sometimes met in the darkness, and who invariably scrutinized pedestrians on Park Street, seemed symbolic, of this attitude. On rare occasions, when in town, the financier dined out, limiting himself to a few houses.

Once in a long while he attended what are known as banquets, such as those given by the Chamber of Commerce, though he generally refused to speak. Hodder, through Mr. Parr's intervention, had gone to one of these, ably

and breezily presided over by the versatile Mr. Plimpton.

Hodder felt not only curiosity and sympathy, but a vexing sense of the fruitlessness of his visits to Park Street. Mr. Parr seemed to like to have him there. And the very fact that the conversation rarely took any vital turn oddly contributed to the increasing permanence of the lien. To venture on any topic relating to the affairs of the day were merely to summon forth the banker's dogmatism, and Hodder's own opinions on such matters were now in a strange and unsettled state. Mr. Parr liked best to talk of his treasures, and of the circumstances during his trips abroad that had led to their acquirement. Once the banker had asked him about parish house matters.

"I'm told you're working very hard— stirring up McCrae. He needs it."

"I'm only trying to study the situation," Hodder replied. "I don't think you quite do justice to McCrae," he added; "he's very faithful, and seems to understand those people thoroughly."

Mr. Parr smiled.

"And what conclusions have you come to? If you think the system should be enlarged and reorganized I am willing at any time to go over it with you, with a view to making an additional contribution. Personally, while I have sympathy for the unfortunate, I'm not at all sure that much of the energy and money put into the institutional work of churches isn't wasted."

"I haven't come to any conclusions— yet," said the rector, with a touch of sadness. "Perhaps I demand too much—expect too much."

The financier, deep in his leather chair under the shaded light, the tips of his fingers pressed together, regarded the younger man thoughtfully, but the smile lingered in his eyes.

"I told you you would meet problems," he said.

**II**

Hodder's cosmos might have been compared, indeed, to that set forth in the Ptolemaic theory of the ancients. Like a cleverly carved Chinese object of ivory in the banker s collection, it was a sys-

tem of spheres, touching, concentric, yet separate. In an outer space swung Mr. Parr; then came the scarcely less rarefied atmosphere of the Constables and Atterburys, Fergusons, Plimptons, Langmaids, Prestons, Larrabbees, Greys, and Gores, and then a smaller sphere which claims but a passing mention. There were, in the congregation of St. John's, a few people of moderate means whose houses or apartments the rector visited; people to whom modern life was increasingly perplexing.

In these ranks were certain maiden ladies and widows who found in church work an outlet to an otherwise circumscribed existence. Hodder met them continually in his daily rounds. There were people like the Bradleys, who rented half a pew and never missed a Sunday; Mr. Bradley, an elderly man whose children had scattered, was an upper clerk in one of Mr. Parr's trust companies: there were bachelors and young women, married or single, who taught in the Sunday school or helped with the night classes. For the most part, all of these mentioned above belonged to an element that once had had a comfortable and well-recognized place in the community, yet had somehow been displaced. Many of them were connected by blood with more fortunate parishioners, but economic pressure had scattered them throughout new neighbourhoods and suburbs. Tradition still bound them to St. John's.

With no fixed orbit, the rector cut at random through all of these strata, and into a fourth. Not very far into it, for this apparently went down to limitless depths, the very contemplation of which made him dizzy. The parish house seemed to float precariously on its surface.

Owing partly to the old-fashioned ideas of Dr. Gilman, and partly to the conservatism of its vestry, the institutionalism of St. John's was by no means up to date. No settlement house, with day nurseries, was maintained in the slums. The parish house, built in the, early nineties, had its gymnasium hall and class and reading rooms, but was not what in these rapidly moving times would be called modern. Presiding over its activities, and seconded by a pale, but earnest young man recently ordained, was Hodder's first assistant, the Reverend Mr. McCrae.

McCrae was another puzzle. He was fifty and gaunt, with a wide flat forehead and thinning, grey hair, and wore steel spectacles. He had a numerous family. His speech, of which he was sparing, bore strong traces of a Caledonian accent. And this, with the addition of the fact that he was painstaking and methodical in his duties, and that his sermons were orthodox in the sense that they were extremely non-committal, was all that Hodder knew about him for many months. He never doubted, however, the man's sincerity and loyalty.

But McCrae had a peculiar effect on him, and as time went on, his conviction deepened that his assistant was watching him. The fact that this tacit criticism did not seem unkindly did not greatly alleviate the impatience that he felt from time to time. He had formed a higher estimate of McCrae's abilities than that generally prevailing throughout the parish; and in spite of, perhaps because of his attitude, was drawn toward the man. This attitude, as Hodder analyzed it from the expressions he occasionally surprised on his assistant's face, was one of tolerance and experience, contemplating, with a faint amusement and a certain regret, the wasteful expenditure of youthful vitality. Yet it involved more. McCrae looked as if he knew— knew many things that he deemed it necessary for the new rector to find out by experience.

But he was a difficult man to talk to.

If the truth be told, the more Hodder became absorbed in these activities of the parish house, the greater grew his perplexity, the more acute his feeling of incompleteness; or rather, his sense that the principle was somehow fundamentally at fault. Out of the waters of the proletariat they fished, assiduously and benignly, but at random, strange specimens! brought them, as it were, blinking to the light, and held them by sheer struggling. And sometimes, when they

slipped away, dived after them. The young curate, Mr. Tompkinson, for the most part did the diving; or, in scriptural language, the searching after the lost sheep.

The results accomplished seemed indeed, as Mr. Parr had remarked, strangely disproportionate to the efforts, for they laboured abundantly. The Italian mothers appeared stolidly appreciative of the altruism of Miss Ramsay, who taught the kindergarten, in taking their charges off their hands for three hours of a morning, and the same might be said of the Jews and Germans and Russians. The newsboys enjoyed the gymnasium and reading-rooms: some of them were drafted into the choir, yet the singing of Te Deums failed somehow to accomplish the miracle of regeneration. The boys, as a rule, were happier, no doubt; the new environments not wholly without results. But the rector was an idealist.

He strove hard to become their friend, and that of the men; to win their confidence, and with a considerable measure of success. On more than one occasion he threw aside his clerical coat and put on boxing-gloves, and he gave a series of lectures, with lantern slides, collected during the six months he had once spent in Europe. The Irish-Americans and the Germans were the readiest to respond, and these were for the most part young workingmen and youths by no means destitute. When they were out of a place, he would often run across them in the reading-room or sitting among the lockers beside the gymnasium, and they would rise and talk to him cordially and even familiarly about their affairs. They liked and trusted him—on a tacit condition. There was a boundary he might not cross. And the existence of that boundary did not seem to trouble McCrae.

One night as he stood with his assistant in the hall after the men had gone, Hodder could contain himself no longer.

"Look here, McCrae," he broke out, "these men never come to church—or only a very few of them."

"No more they do," McCrae agreed.

"Why don't they?"

"Ye've asked them, perhaps."

"I've spoken to one or two of them," admitted the rector.

"And what do they tell you?"

Hodder smiled.

"They don't tell me anything. They dodge."

"Precisely," said McCrae.

"We're not making Christians of them," said Hodder, beginning to walk up and down. "Why is it?"

"It's a big question."

"It is a big question. It's the question of all questions, it seems to me. The function of the Church, in my opinion, is to make Christians."

"Try to teach them religion," said McCrae—he almost pronounced it releegion—"and see what happens. Ye'll have no classes at all. They only come, the best of them, because ye let them alone that way, and they get a little decency and society help. It's somewhat to keep them out of the dance-halls and saloons maybe."

"It's not enough," the rector asserted. "You've had a great deal of experience with them. And I want to know why, in your view, more of them don't come into the Church."

"Would ye put Jimmy Flanagan and Otto Bauer and Tony Baldassaro in Mr. Parr's pew?" McCrae inquired, with a slight flavour of irony that was not ill-natured. "Or perhaps Mrs. Larrabbee would make room for them?"

"I've considered that, of course," replied Hodder, thoughtfully, though he was a little surprised that McCrae should have mentioned it. "You think their reasons are social, then,—that they feel the gap. I feel it myself most strongly. And yet none of these men are Socialists. If they were, they wouldn't come here to the parish house."

"They're not Socialists," agreed McCrae.

"But there is room in the back and sides of the church, and there is the early service and the Sunday night service, when the pews are free. Why don't they come to these?"

"Religion doesn't appeal to them."

"Why not?"

"Ye've asked me a riddle. All I know is that the minute ye begin to preach, off they go and never come back."

Hodder, with unconscious fixity, looked into his assistant's honest face. He had an exasperating notion that Mc-Crae might have said more, if he would.

"Haven't you a theory?"

"Try yourself," said McCrae. His manner was abrupt, yet oddly enough, not ungracious.

"Don't think I'm criticizing," said the rector, quickly.

"I know well ye're not."

"I've been trying to learn. It seems to me that we are only accomplishing half our task, and I know that St. John's is not unique in this respect. I've been talking to Andrews, of Trinity, about their poor."

"Does he give you a remedy?"

"No," Hodder said. "He can't see any more than I can why Christianity doesn't appeal any longer. The fathers and mothers of these people went to church, in the old country and in this. Of course he sees, as you and I do, that society has settled into layers, and that the layers won't mix. And he seems to agree with me that there is a good deal of energy exerted for a comparatively small return."

"I understand that's what Mr. Parr says."

These references to Mr. Parr disturbed Hodder. He had sometimes wondered, when he had been compelled to speak about his visits to the financier, how McCrae regarded them. He was sure that McCrae did regard them.

"Mr. Parr is willing to be even more generous than he has been," Hodder said. "The point is, whether it's wise to enlarge our scope on the present plan. What do you think?"

"Ye can reach more," McCrae spoke without enthusiasm.

"What's the use of reaching them, only to touch them? In addition to being helped materially and socially, and kept away from the dance-halls and saloons, they ought to be fired by the Gospels, to be remade. They should be going out into the highways and byways to bring others into the church."

The Scotchman's face changed a little. For an instant his eyes lighted up, whether in sympathy or commiseration or both, Hodder could not tell.

"I'm with ye, Mr. Hodder, if ye'll show me the way. But oughtn't we to begin at both ends?"

"At both ends?" Hodder repeated.

"Surely. With the people in the pews? Oughtn't we to be firing them, too?"

"Yes," said the rector. "You're right."

He turned away, to feel McCrae's hand on his sleeve.

"Maybe it will come, Mr. Hodder," he said. "There's no telling when the light will strike in."

It was the nearest to optimism he had ever known his assistant to approach.

"McCrae," he asked, "have you ever tried to do anything with Dalton Street?"

"Dalton Street?"

The real McCrae, whom he had seemed to see emerging, retired abruptly, presenting his former baffling and noncommittal exterior.

"Yes," Hodder forced himself to go on, and it came to him that he had repeated virtually the same words to Mr. Parr, "it is at our very doors, a continual reproach. There is real poverty in those rooming houses, and I have never seen vice so defiant and shameless."

"It's a shifty place, that," McCrae replied. "They're in it one day and gone the next, a sort of catch-basin for all the rubbish of the city. I can recall when decent people lived there, and now it's all light housekeeping and dives and what not."

"But that doesn't relieve us of responsibility," Hodder observed.

"I'm not denying it. I think ye'll find there's very little to get hold of."

Once more, he had the air of stopping short, of being able to say more.

Hodder refrained from pressing him.

Dalton Street continued to haunt him. And often at nightfall, as he hurried back to his bright rooms in the parish house from some of the many errands that absorbed his time, he had a feeling of self-accusation as he avoided women wearily treading the pavements, or girls and children plodding homeward through the wet, wintry streets. Some glanced at him with heavy eyes, others passed sullenly, with bent heads. At such moments his sense of helplessness was overpowering. He could not follow them to the dreary dwellings where they lodged.

Eldon Parr had said that poverty was inevitable.

CPSIA information can be obtained at www.ICGtesting.com
Printed in the USA
BVOW00s2040201113

336859BV00018B/579/P